Kealy Connor Lonr

H.OPE

Illustrator Lora Look

1

When days are hard and long,
I hope that you are strong.

2

3

When choices seem so tough,
I hope you're wise enough.

5

When times are glum and dark,

I hope you find your spark.

7

And even though you're stressed,
I hope that you feel blessed.

9

When sadness comes your way,

I hope that joy will stay.

11

12

When loneliness is real,
I hope it's love you feel.

GET WELL SOON!

13

And when you are afraid,
I hope that you have prayed.

14

15

16

When others fall behind,
I hope that you are kind.

When helping friends in need,
I hope you're brave and lead.

When trouble's all around,
I hope beauty can be found.

21

22

And when you go outside,
I hope wonder is your guide.

23

24

When work becomes a trial,
I hope that you can smile.

When waiting for your chance,

I hope you get to dance.

28

When passion comes to you.

I hope your dreams come true.

And...
when life is crazy wild,
I hope for peace, my child.

31

FUN FACTS FROM THE AUTHOR:

**All of my six children are featured in this book. They are all about the same age in the illustrations.

**The other children are based on friends and neighbors of our youngest child/daughter.

**Our dogs are in this book. Seamus spent her years with our four older kids. Presley is sharing her life, mainly with our two youngest girls.

**I had my amazing illustrator include some things from nature, that have special symbols and meanings to match the themes in my book. Here are some of them:

**The two mourning doves are a symbol of FREEDOM and PEACE. These birds/a couple, usually stay together for life.

**The two eggs in the nest show HOPE and PURITY.

**The eggs hatched, and the two baby birds in the nest symbolize NEW LIFE and HAPPINESS.

**Butterflies can mean CHANGE, BEAUTY, HOPE, LUCK, LOVE, and LIFE.

**Types of flowers that represent HOPE are the Iris, Hyacinth, Gladiolus, and yellow tulips.

**Flowers for LOVE are red roses, red tulips, asters, and daisies.

**Some flowers for PEACE are white poppies, lavender, violets, and peonies.

**The star means to reach for DREAMS, and always have HOPE.

**The Earth ball on the back cover of the book, shows PEACE, LOVE, and HOPE for the world.

**Rainbows are a symbol of LOVE, LUCK, and HOPE.

For my first family--my amazing mom and dad, Micki and Jim, and two younger sisters, Kerry and Kathy, who taught me so much about life. Our parents gave us a glorious childhood, filled with unconditional love, compassion, literacy, learning, and fun. They modeled how to be strong, positive, humble, kind, and brave. Our mom and dad taught us to notice our blessings, look for beauty, to dance, and to pray. We learned to care for people, animals, and the Earth. So thankful they gave us courage, confidence, and hope. Our parents made unbelievable sacrifices, so that we could follow our dreams! They forever inspire me to defend the oppressed, celebrate diversity, and have a grateful heart.

For my sister, Kerry, who helped me revise and edit this book. I am thankful for her genuine, loving support, honest feedback, and great ideas. She is always willing to take time to help me. So lucky to have her in my life!

Dedication

For my husband, Greg, who encourages and motivates me to use my gifts, and find my strength. So glad that he helps me see the positive in everything, and shares his wise advice. Greg is the first one to hear my stories. He is a patient listener, and we brainstorm ideas. Greg is like superman, a selfless giver, was destined to coach, and to raise kids! So grateful for all of the time he spends with our kids, giving me time to be an author. Greg helps us all learn to use grit to succeed. Two of his favorite words are: "Keep going!"

For my six beautiful, awesome children, who inspire me to write children's books. Seeing the world through their eyes, reminded me that simple wonders of childhood are magical. Their dad and I enjoyed watching their personalities and passions unfold. We are blessed to be their parents, and they are our legacy. Our kids are all multi-talented, and we are super proud! We have raised them to be strong, kind, brave, and grateful. Letting them grow up is bittersweet, but we hope that they will chase their dreams, and change the world!
Love them--"our champions"--Connor, Moran, Gable, Gara, Summer, and Shanae!

Like the book?
Please consider
leaving a review
online.

Available on
Amazon.com

Facebook/Instagram:
AuthorKealyConnorLonning
KealyConnor0716@gmail.com

Books by Kealy Connor Lonning

Follow Your Dreams

The Wonders of Childhood

To receive updates, book releases, and special offers, visit
KealyConnorLonning.com

Made in United States
Troutdale, OR
01/27/2024

17209934R00024